The Sing-Song of Old Man KANGAROO

Find out more about

Rudyard Kipling's

JUST So STORIES

at Shoo Rayner's fabulous website,

www.shoo-rayner.co.uk

First published in 2007 by Orchard Books
First paperback publication in 2008

ORCHARD BOOKS
338 Euston Road, London NW1 3BH
Orchard Books Australia
Level 17/207 Kent St, Sydney, NSW 2000

ISBN 978 1 84616 412 5

A CIP catalogue record for this book is available from the British Library.

3 5 7 9 10 8 6 4 2

Printed in Great Britain by CPI Bookmarque, Croydon

Orchard Books is a division of Hachette Children's Books,
an Hachette UK company.

www.orchardbooks.co.uk

Rudyard Kipling's
JUST SO STORIES

The Sing-Song of Old Man KANGAROO

Retold and illustrated by
SHOO RAYNER

ORCHARD BOOKS

Long, long ago, at the very beginning of time, when everything was just getting sorted out, the Kangaroo was quite a Different Animal to the one we know now.

He was grey and he was
woolly, and his pride was
inordinate. With his four short
legs, he danced on an outcrop in the
middle of Australia.

Back in those days, there were Jinns and Angels and other kinds of spirits, who were put in charge of sorting out the world. So Kangaroo went to see the Spirit, Nqa.

He went to Nqa at six
before breakfast, saying,
"Make me different from
all other Animals by five
this afternoon."

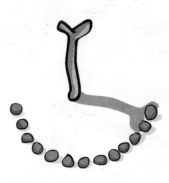

Nqa jumped up
from his seat on the
sandflat and shouted,
"Go away!"

7

Kangaroo was grey and he was woolly, and his pride was inordinate. He danced on a rock-ledge in the middle of Australia,

then he went to see the Spirit, Nquing.

8

Inordinate Pride

Inordinate: unusually large or excessive.

Pride: having a high opinion of oneself or of one's achievements.

Pride always comes before a fall –
Kangaroos please take note.

He went to Nquing at eight after breakfast, saying, "Make me different from all other Animals, and also make me wonderfully popular by five this afternoon."

Nquing jumped up
from his burrow in the
spinifex and shouted,
"Go away!"

Kangaroo was grey
and he was woolly,
and his pride was
inordinate. He danced
on a sandbank in the
middle of Australia,
then he went to the
Spirit, Nqong.

He went to Nqong at ten
before lunchtime, saying,
"Make me different from
other Animals.

"Make me popular
too, so they'll all want
to follow me, and do it
by five this afternoon."

Nqong jumped up from his bath in the salt-pan and shouted, "Yes, I will!"

Nqong called Dingo – Yellow-Dog Dingo, who was hungry and dusty in the sunshine, and showed him Kangaroo.

13

Nqong said, "Dingo! Wake up, Dingo! Do you see that gentleman dancing on the sand? He wants to be popular so Animals will follow him. Dingo, make him so!"

Up jumped Dingo – Yellow-Dog
Dingo, always hungry and grinning
like a steak-knife. He said, "What,
that cat-rabbit?"

Off ran Dingo – Yellow-Dog Dingo,
after that proud Kangaroo. And off
went the Kangaroo on his four little
legs like a bunny.

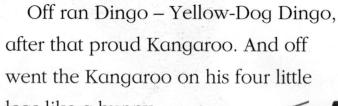

Kangaroo
ran through
the desert.

He ran
through the
mountains.

He ran
through the
salt-pans.

He ran
through the
reed-beds.

He ran
through the
blue gums.

He ran
through the
spinifex.

He ran till his
front legs ached
and ached.
He had to!

Still ran Dingo – Yellow-Dog Dingo,
always hungry, grinning like a rat-trap,
never getting nearer, never getting farther,
but always running after Kangaroo.

He had to!

Some Things Kangaroo Ran Through

Saltpans

When pools of water
dry out in the sun,
salt is left behind.

Blue gums

Blue gums are a kind
of eucalyptus tree.
Eucalyptus oil helps
clear stuffy noses.

Spinifex

Sometimes called porcupine grass,
spinifex leaves are stiff, sharp and pointy.

Still ran Kangaroo –
Old Man Kangaroo.
He ran through
the tea-trees.

He ran through
the mulga.

He ran
through the
long grass.

He ran
through the
short grass.

He ran
through the
Tropics of
Capricorn
and Cancer.

He ran till his
hind legs ached.
He had to!

24

The Tropics of Capricorn and Cancer

The Tropics of Capricorn and Cancer
are imaginary lines that circle the earth
north and south of the equator.

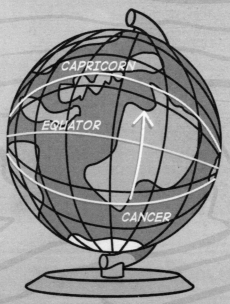

Long, long ago, when everything was just
getting sorted out, the equator ran through
the middle of Australia, but Australia
has since moved south.

Still ran Dingo – Yellow-Dog Dingo,
hungrier and hungrier, grinning like
a snap-dragon,

never getting nearer,
never getting farther, till they
came to the Wollgong River.

Now, there wasn't any bridge, and there wasn't any ferry-boat, and Kangaroo didn't know how to get over, so he stood on his legs and he hopped.

He had to!

How to Cross a River Without a Bridge

If the current is weak – swim.

Float on a dead branch.

Take a running jump.

Swing on a vine.

He hopped
through the
Flinders.

He hopped
through the
Cinders.

He hopped
through the
deserts in the
middle of
Australia.

He hopped like
a Kangaroo.

First he hopped
a metre, then he
hopped three.

His legs were growing stronger, his legs were growing longer, until he hopped four metres, ninety-three!

He hadn't any time for rest or refreshment, and he wanted them very much.

Still ran Dingo – Yellow-Dog Dingo,
very much bewildered, very much
hungry, and wondering what in the
world or out of it made Old Man
Kangaroo hop.

For he hopped
like a cricket,

or corn that
is popping,

or a shiny new
ball on a hard,
stone floor.

He had to!

He tucked up his front legs. He hopped on his hind legs. He stuck out his tail for a balance-weight behind him, and he hopped through the Darling Downs.

He had to!

Still ran Dingo – Tired-Dog Dingo, hungrier and hungrier, very much bewildered, and wondering when in the world or out of it Old Man Kangaroo would stop.

Then came Nqong from his
bath in the salt-pans, and said,
"It's five o'clock."

Down sat Dingo – Poor Dog Dingo,
always hungry and dusty in the sunshine.
He hung out his tongue and howled.

Down sat Kangaroo – Old Man Kangaroo. He stuck out his tail like a milking-stool behind him, and said, "Thank goodness that's finished!"

Then said Nqong, who was always a gentleman, "Why aren't you grateful to Yellow-Dog Dingo? Why don't you thank him for all he has done for you?"

Then said Kangaroo – Tired Old Kangaroo, "He's chased me out of the homes of my childhood. He's chased me out of my regular meal-times. He's altered my shape so I'll never get it back, and he's played Old Scratch with my legs."

Then said Nqong,
"Perhaps I'm mistaken, but
didn't you ask me to make
you different from all other
Animals, as well as to make
you popular and followed?
And now it is five o'clock."

"Yes," said Kangaroo. "But I wish
that I hadn't. I thought you would do it
by charms and incantations, but this has
been a practical joke."

"A joke!" said Nqong from his bath in the blue gums. "Say that again and I'll whistle up Dingo to chase you and run your hind legs off."

"No," said the Kangaroo. "I must apologise. Legs are legs, and you needn't alter them as far as I am concerned. I only meant to explain that I've had nothing to eat since morning, and I'm very empty indeed."

"Yes," said Dingo – Yellow-Dog Dingo. "I am in the same situation. I've made him different from all other Animals, but what can I have for my tea?"

Then said Nqong from his bath in the salt-pans, "Come back and ask me tomorrow, because now I'm going to wash my hair."

So they were left, right there, in the
middle of Australia. Old Man Kangaroo
and Yellow-Dog Dingo stared at each
other and each of them said, "It's all
your fault!"

Rudyard Kipling's
JUST SO STORIES

Retold and illustrated by
SHOO RAYNER

All priced at £3.99

Rudyard Kipling's Just So Stories are available from all good bookshops,
or can be ordered direct from
the publisher: Orchard Books, PO BOX 29, Douglas IM99 1BQ
Credit card orders please telephone 01624 836000
or fax 01624 837033 or visit our internet site: www.orchardbooks.co.uk
or e-mail: bookshop@enterprise.net for details.

To order please quote title, author and ISBN
and your full name and address.
Cheques and postal orders should be made payable to 'Bookpost plc.'
Postage and packing is FREE within the UK
(overseas customers should add £2.00 per book).

Prices and availability are subject to change.